HELLO KITTY

and friends

The Summer Fair

HELLO KITTY

and friends

The Summer Fair

HarperCollins *Children's Books*

MEET HELLO KITTY and friends

Hello Kitty

Mimmy

Tammy

Mama

Papa

Grandpa

Grandma

Fifi

Dear Daniel

With special thanks to
Linda Chapman and Michelle Misra

First published in Great Britain by HarperCollins *Children's Books* in 2013

www.harpercollins.co.uk
1 3 5 7 9 10 8 6 4 2
ISBN: 978-000-751437-3

Printed and bound in England by Clays Ltd, St Ives plc.

MIX
Paper from
responsible sources
FSC **FSC™ C007454**
www.fsc.org

FSC™ is a non-profit international organisation established to promote
the responsible management of the world's forests. Products carrying the
FSC label are independently certified to assure consumers that they come
from forests that are managed to meet the social, economic and
ecological needs of present and future generations,
and other controlled sources.

Find out more about HarperCollins and the environment at
www.harpercollins.co.uk/green

Contents

An Exciting Announcement

Hello Kitty stared out of the classroom window.
She'd been doodling a fashion design on her
notebook – a pink top with capped sleeves that
tucked perfectly into pink and white polka-dotted
shorts. It just needed a little something else...

The rest of the class were working hard on their paintings. Miss Davey, Hello Kitty's teacher, called out to them – it was nearly time to finish up and show them to her!

Hello Kitty looked up. She needed to start her painting – just as soon as she had finished off the outfit she was drawing. A butterfly fluttered past the window.

She gasped as a thought popped into her head, and she started to sketch again. When

she stopped, the pink top
had a purple butterfly in
the centre. She smiled.

Perfect!

Fifi, one of Hello
Kitty's closest friends,
leaned over to look at
her sketch. She loved
Hello Kitty's fashion
designs, and was
always excited to see a
new one.

Hello Kitty smiled at her as Fifi checked it
out and told her how cool it was. Super-cool!

But she really needed to start on her painting

for Miss Davey! She shuffled her notebook

away. Her other two friends at the table – Dear

Daniel and Tammy – were hard at work on

their paintings.

Hello Kitty, Dear Daniel, Tammy and Fifi were such good friends they had started a Friendship Club. They had **fun** meetings where they did lots of things like baking, making models and painting, and they also liked to make up rules about friendship.

Hello Kitty put her brush in the green paint pot. Miss Davey had said to paint the thing that made her feel *happiest* in the world. That was easy! Her brush flew across the page. Eventually she looked up.

She had painted herself and all her friends in
the park together. Miss Davey came and looked
over Hello Kitty's shoulder.

Her glossy black hair fell forward as she

looked at the painting and smiled – it was very

good! Hello Kitty turned the paper round so

Miss Davey could see it better. It was of the

Friendship Club of course!

Miss Davey grinned, then clapped her hands together and called out to the class. It was time to clean up, and then she had an announcement to make.

There was excited chatter as chairs scraped back and everyone darted around the classroom. At last the paints were put away, and they all sat down.

Miss Davey started to tell them about her dog.

His name was **Spot.** Hello

Kitty looked at her friends

excitedly as Miss Davey

flashed up a picture of a little

black and white dog on the

whitescreen in front of them.

Miss Davey smiled as she told them all

about how Spot came from Paws, the

local animal rescue centre. She clicked up

another picture and another, until a poodle,

a bulldog, and a scruffy looking

brown-and-white dog sat beside

Spot on the screen. All the dogs

came from Paws, she explained, which rescued them and found them new homes. And the next weekend, she was helping organise a fair to help raise money for Paws! Everyone called out excitedly.

What would happen at the fair? Could they all go?

Excited questions filled the air.

Miss Davey smiled at their enthusiasm – of course they could all go! The more people there were, the more money they might raise. There would be lots of things happening, although they hadn't decided what yet. One of the ideas was to release lots of balloons at the same time, with the rescue centre's name and a message about helping animals inside them. People would buy them to let them all go together – it would look very impressive.

That sounded *amazing!*

Everyone started talking at once.

Miss Davey smiled at the class, and held her hands up for quiet. What they really needed were some more fundraising ideas – and she was hoping the class might be able to help out with that!

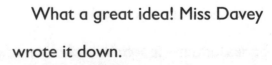

Fifi stuck up her hand immediately – what about a **bouncy** castle?

What a great idea! Miss Davey wrote it down.

Tammy suggested a book stall. She loved books.

Bouncy castle
Book stall
Face painting
Model-making stall

Face painting was Hello Kitty's idea as she joined in excitedly.

Dear Daniel called out too; they could have a model-making stall! The ideas were coming thick and fast.

Miss Davey laughed, and asked everyone to slow down; there were lots of good ideas, but she couldn't write them down quickly enough!

But then Hello Kitty had an especially good idea. They could have a baking competition, and sell the entries afterwards!

Mama was brilliant at baking – Hello Kitty was sure she'd enter.

Miss Davey thought it was a great idea. At that moment, the bell went for break. That would do for now, she told them, as they had given her some fantastic ideas. But for now, it was break time – time to go outside and play!

Everyone rushed out, talking **excitedly** about the fair. Hello Kitty and her friends hung back to see if they could help Miss Davey tidy away the rest of the art things.

Miss Davey thanked them as they cleared up. The four of them were always helpful, and she appreciated it. In fact, she asked, they wouldn't like to help out at the fair, would they?

Hello Kitty gasped. She'd **l♥ve** to! She looked at her friends to see what they thought, and they all nodded eagerly. All four of them turned to Miss Davey and smiled.

Miss Davey beamed back at them, and said maybe they could organise the stalls they had suggested. Would the Friendship Club be up for the challenge?

Hello Kitty, Fifi, Tammy and Dear Daniel grinned at each other. They sure would – you could always count on the Friendship Club!

Making Plans

Helping at the summer fair was all the friends

could talk about as they spilled out of the

classroom after helping tidy away.

Dear Daniel was keen to start organising.

They would be able to make some proper

plans after school, at their next Friendship Club meeting.

Hello Kitty agreed; thank goodness he'd reminded her! She'd nearly forgotten about it.

Fifi giggled, and asked how could Hello Kitty forget their meeting – it was at her house! They hadn't yet decided what everyone would bring though.

Tammy thought hard, and suggested pens and paper. They were always helpful. But they should make sure they were **sparkly!** Hello Kitty laughed.

They should all bring sparkly ideas too! And don't forget your membership cards, they reminded each other. This meeting was going to be so much **fun!**

Hello Kitty could hardly sit still that afternoon, she was so excited. When Mama came to pick up her and her twin sister Mimmy from school, she couldn't wait to tell them all about the fair.

Mama chuckled as the two sisters jumped

into the car. Hello Kitty was chattering away **excitedly**, telling them all about the fair; she was talking so quickly that Mama had to ask her to slow down! Mama thought it was great that Hello Kitty had been asked to help. She wanted to know all the details; it was going to have stalls and things, was it?

Hello Kitty nodded, and was telling her all
about it when she remembered that she had
said Mama would enter the baking competition!
She asked her now – would she please? Her
Apple Pie was Hello Kitty's favourite.

Mama raised her eyebrows and smiled. Of course she would enter, she said, and she'd help them with anything the Friendship Club needed. She knew that Hello Kitty and her friends loved organising things and helping out. Mimmy said she would to go to the fair with Alice, who was one of her friends from class. They would tell everyone they knew about it too, so lots more people would come.

Hello Kitty smiled gratefully at her. She really wanted the fair to be a success and raise lots of money for Paws.

When they got home and went inside, the smell of freshly-made cookies wafted towards them. Delicious! Hello Kitty put her rucksack away and sniffed the air deeply, then turned to look at Mama. The cookies were for their meeting, Mama explained. She had thought they might be hungry – and she was right! Especially for **cookies.**

Hello Kitty thanked her, and called out to Mimmy – did she want to join the meeting? Mimmy sometimes came along and joined in with the Friendship Club.

But Mimmy said she was going to practise playing her flute. It wasn't long now till her next exam. Hello Kitty nodded. Mimmy loved playing musical instruments. It was good that they liked different things, as well as the stuff they liked to do together!

Hello Kitty went to the kitchen and got out her pencil case. She had a watermelon rubber, a *glitter* pen, and a bow-shaped pencil sharpener. She stuck up a big piece of paper on the wall and got a felt tip pen for writing a list.

Then she waited for the others to arrive.

Luckily, she didn't have long to wait. Dear Daniel, Fifi and Tammy were soon dropped off by their parents, and soon they were all sitting around the table, tucking into the still-warm cookies.

Hello Kitty suggested they start by making

a list of what they were going to do at the

fair. Then they would be able to work out who

would run each stall!

She started the list on the big piece of paper.

FRIENDSHIP CLUB STALLS

Bouncy Castle

Books

Face Painting

Model-making

Who wanted to start? Hello Kitty looked around at her friends.

Dear Daniel thought Fifi should do the bouncy castle, as it was her idea, *and* she was sporty.

Fifi thought that was a **great** idea, and agreed enthusiastically. She'd love to! But she said she'd happily do face painting or look after the books if someone else wanted to do the bouncy castle.

Dear Daniel didn't mind what he did. He was

happy with anything! But he wondered aloud,

what did Tammy want to do?

Tammy didn't mind either – she just wanted

to help try and raise lots of

money for Paws.

Hello Kitty scratched

her head. This was

tricky. How would

they decide when no

one would say what

they wanted to do? But

then she had an **idea!** What

if they wrote a list of everyone's talents and

then matched each person up to a stall? They could write it in different colours. Pink for Hello Kitty, purple for Fifi, **red for Dear Daniel** and blue for Tammy!

Everyone thought a list was a great idea. Hello Kitty wrote up their names.

Fifi started. Hello Kitty first… hmmm, what should they write? She was brilliant at organising things. Fifi took the pink pen and wrote 'organised' under Hello Kitty's name.

Hello Kitty agreed eagerly, and took the pen back as Fifi offered it to her. What else could they write?

Dear Daniel suggested that she was great at telling them what to do.

And Tammy called out that she was always super-stylish!

Hello Kitty looked puzzled. She liked that Tammy had said she was stylish, but wasn't sure about the rest; it sounded like they thought she was a bit bossy! Was she really like that she asked?

Her friends nodded.

Hmmm. OK then, said Hello Kitty – what about Fifi's talents?

Tammy said Fifi was brave.

Loud was Dear Daniel's suggestion!

Hello Kitty added energetic, and wrote them all down. She smiled. Fifi was definitely loud and energetic!

She glanced round. Fifi looked surprised, and said she wasn't *that* loud, was she? Hello Kitty assured her that she might be, but it was *great!* They all liked her like that.

Dear Daniel picked up the blue pen. It was time for Tammy's talents! She was good at thinking up

tricks, and good at listening. He wrote them
both down.

Hello Kitty said fun, but also kind and gentle.
Into reading was Fifi's suggestion.

Tammy looked worried.
Apart from the tricks, she
didn't think she sounded
like she was *much* fun. The
others insisted of course
she was fun, but Tammy
wasn't convinced.

Dear Daniel turned back to the
list. What about him?

The three others called out. He was practical!

Sensible!

And good at making things, was the final suggestion.

Oh no! Dear Daniel thought he sounded boring.

Hello Kitty began to feel this wasn't such a good idea after all. All the things they had said were meant to be compliments but her friends were starting to look unsure. Maybe the list wasn't helping! It was time to do something else instead.

But Fifi pointed out that they still needed to decide what stalls they were going to run! Hello Kitty started to speak, but stopped herself. She'd been about to say that they should all just say their **favourite** stall but she didn't want to sound bossy. Hmmm... So instead, she asked if anyone else had any ideas.

They looked at each other.

Dear Daniel had an idea. They *could* just put the stall names in a bowl and whoever pulled a stall out got to run it. But they would all have to stick with what they got – no swapping or they'd never agree!

Everyone nodded.

Dear Daniel wrote the names down on pieces of paper, put them into a bowl and handed them round. They each picked one and read them.

Tammy had picked the bouncy castle.

Dear Daniel had the face painting.

Fifi had the model-making.

And Hello Kitty

had chosen the

book stall, which

wouldn't have been

her first choice. She'd rather have

had the face painting or bouncy castle.

But at least it was settled! So that was good.

Fifi agreed. She turned to Hello Kitty and

asked what they should do. Could they play a

game now? Did she have any ideas?

Hello Kitty could think of lots of things but

bouncy castle

model-making

face painting

book stall

she didn't say them; she didn't want to seem bossy. Did anyone else have any good ideas?

There was a silence.

Fifi suggested they could turn cartwheels! And maybe… She stopped, then started again. What about something quiet instead? Like drawing or making up a story. She liked quiet things.

But Tammy thought cartwheels sounded fun, and said so loudly. They should do something **crazy!**

Dear Daniel agreed —
they *should* do cartwheels!
And stand on their heads
too! He jumped up.

Hello Kitty blinked. Her
friends weren't acting like
themselves at all! She wasn't
sure there was room for them to do cartwheels
and headstands, and she didn't want them to
hurt themselves.

So what could they do?

It seemed that without Hello Kitty to
organise things, no one could decide! They still
hadn't started anything by the time everyone's

parents arrived to pick them up.

It had been a very strange Friendship Club meeting, Hello Kitty thought as she waved her friends off. Everyone had acted completely out of character. She hoped everyone was going to be back to normal tomorrow!

3

The Friendship Club Meeting

The next morning before class, the four friends

told Miss Davey about their plans. She was

impressed with how quickly they'd organised

themselves. They'd done a great job! She would

let them get on with it since they had it all in

hand, but would be around to help them if they needed her. She hurried off to get ready for the first lesson.

They had loads to do! They planned to have another Friendship Club meeting on Wednesday, to check progress and see how everyone was getting on with their stalls.

They had to make them a *success!* And there would be just three days left until the fair by then.

Hello Kitty gulped. Put like that, it didn't seem long at all!

The Friendship Club met at Hello Kitty's house after school on Wednesday. Hello Kitty was about to start the meeting when she stopped and thought. Perhaps she should let someone else organise the meeting for a change? She sat down and waited for someone else to start instead. Fifi and Dear Daniel started chatting about a football game they'd played at school and Tammy took a book out and started reading. Hello Kitty **wriggled** in her seat as the minutes passed. They had a lot to talk about and she was desperate to start! It was hard to sit still and wait for someone else to take charge.

In the end she couldn't wait any longer. It

was getting late! They should start,
she said. Dear Daniel agreed,
glancing at the clock. They'd
already wasted ten minutes.

Everyone looked
expectantly at Hello
Kitty but she kept silent.
Dear Daniel gave her a
puzzled look – didn't she
want to tell them what
to do?

Hello Kitty gave a small smile, and asked him
why didn't he start this time instead? It shouldn't
always be her.

Dear Daniel swallowed. He wasn't sure about that, but OK! He looked at where Hello Kitty had stuck up the list of stalls, and looked at Tammy. He asked her how the bouncy castle was going. Was everything organised yet?

Tammy said it was going well! Her mum had booked it to be delivered at 10am. She'd made **lots** of tickets, and thought she might bring some books for people to read while they were waiting for their turn.

It sounded **super!** Everyone was really
pleased, and Tammy blushed. Dear Daniel
turned to Hello Kitty to ask about the books for
the book stall.

She had started collecting them, she
explained, and had put posters up at school.

People had been
bringing them in,
and while she
hadn't sorted
them yet, she
would.

Books needed
for the
PAWS
Summer Fair!

Talk to
Hello Kitty
x

Dear Daniel
thought that

was super too! She had done a great job. And how about the model-making, Dear Daniel asked Fifi – did she have everything she needed?

Fifi said she sort of did; she didn't have many materials yet, but she'd made a good start on painting a banner to put up. She'd have things to make the models with by the fair; something would **definitely** turn up! Dear Daniel smiled at her, but he looked worried. Then he brightened up. He had an idea to help them, he explained; what if they made a list of everything they still needed to do?

Fifi didn't look very happy with the idea of making a list. Wouldn't that be a bit boring? Dear Daniel went pink. It might be a bit boring, he said — they should just move on.

Tammy didn't agree though; Hello Kitty always made lists! And they were always helpful! Hello Kitty wanted to say that lists were **really** useful when you were organising something but she didn't want to seem bossy. She did like lists, but they didn't have to have one if the others didn't think so, so she kept quiet.

So it was decided – they would forget the list! Dear Daniel looked at them all nervously.

Hello Kitty smiled at him. Everything would be fine!

And Fifi smiled at everyone! They shouldn't worry, she said – everything would be great on Saturday. They would just have to wait and see.

Hello Kitty had **butterflies** in her tummy. She hoped Fifi was right!

4

The Big Day Arrives!

By the day before the fair, Hello Kitty had collected **lots** of books. She had planned to sort them into boxes to help her take them to the stall but every time she started going through them she was distracted by drawing a new fashion design or by helping Mama. By

Friday afternoon, her bedroom was so full of

books that she could barely see the floor!

Mama put her to bed that night and kissed

her on the forehead, wishing her a good night.

Hello Kitty looked across at the leggings and pink and white **sparkly** top she'd laid out to wear. It was so exciting to think of the fair the next day. How was she ever going to get to sleep?

But somehow she did. The next morning dawned *bright* and sunny. Hello Kitty got up early to help Papa load the books into the car. He would take them to Paws, the animal centre, and help set up the stalls. He patted her on the head and said he'd see her later.

He reminded her to make sure she ate a good
breakfast before he went out the door. It was
going to be a long day! Hello Kitty waved
goodbye to him and skipped back inside. The
smell of pancakes wafted through the air. Mama
was cooking one of her special breakfasts –

Yum!

Later that morning, Mama dropped Hello Kitty off at Paws. The fair was taking place in one of its fields. Mama would be back later with Grandma and Grandpa, Papa and Mimmy. She wished Hello Kitty good luck with setting up her book stall.

Hello Kitty thanked Mama, and watched her drive away. She felt **excitement** shoot through her. She might not be running her ideal stall but there wasn't a cloud in the sky, and it was going to be a **SUPER** day! Banners

were hanging from the entrance and lots of

stallholders were already unpacking boxes.

Hello Kitty spotted Tammy standing next to

the bouncy castle, and called out to her.

A group of younger children who had come with the stallholders had already gathered, and they were all trying to *leap* on to the castle. Tammy was rushing around like crazy, trying to get them to wait for their turns!

Bouncy Castle

But the children weren't paying any attention. She was calling out **loudly** to try and be heard over them. They might hurt themselves if they all got on at once!

Hello Kitty ran over to help her. She clapped her hands, and spoke loudly and clearly to all the children — they needed to listen to Tammy, and wait their

turn! Otherwise they would have to turn the
whole bouncy castle off, and no one would get
to have a go! She smiled at them all, and she
and Tammy both held their hands
out to them so they
could get off the
castle and form a
proper queue.

The children did
as she said and climbed off the castle, forming
a line. Still smiling, Hello Kitty told them the
rules. Four of them on at a time, and after five
minutes Tammy would let them know their time
was up and they could swap over.

Phew! Tammy was so relieved. She thanked Hello Kitty as the first four children got on and started bouncing.

Hello Kitty waved at her as she raced away. She needed to find her stall if it was going to be ready in time!

She set off across the field. Fifi was standing by her stall pinning up a banner saying 'MODEL MAKING.' It was painted in big swirly letters and looked great.

Hello Kitty ran over to her and told her how amazing the banner looked. But Fifi looked a bit unsure as she thanked her.

The trouble was she'd spent so long making

the banner, she hadn't got many model-making

materials. She had been hoping there might

be some stuff she could use at the fair! She

looked round at what she had and looked a bit

lost. She had some paint and glue and pipe

cleaners, but not much else. Hello Kitty patted

her on the back to reassure her.

Fifi looked at Hello Kitty – could she please

help?

Hello Kitty really wanted to but she still had

the book stall to set up. She would come back

and help as soon as she had sorted the books out, she promised. But while she was doing that, she'd think about where they could find some materials to make models with. Fifi smiled her thanks.

Hello Kitty hurried on. Dear Daniel's face painting stall was very near her book stall. She saw him sorting out the face paints.

He called out when he saw her. He'd been waiting for her to arrive – he really needed her *help!* He had no idea what designs to paint on people's faces. He'd been going to invent

them on the spot, but now that he had arrived he was panicking. It was much harder than he had thought it would be! He wasn't even sure how to **USE** face paint. Hello Kitty was brilliant with things like this – please would she help him?

Hello Kitty smiled at him. Of course she would! But she'd also said she'd help Fifi too, and check Tammy was OK with the bouncy castle, *and* she still had to get the book stall done! But she would come back and help him as soon as her stall was ready.

Dear Daniel nodded and thanked her, smiling.

Hello Kitty ran on to her stall, her heart beating fast. The morning was going to be *really* busy! What were they all going to do?

5

Taking Charge

Papa had put out all the boxes of books by the book stall. Hello Kitty started to unpack them as quickly as she could. How should she organise them? She tried by subject first but it didn't look very exciting. What about organising

them by colour? She put the purple books
on one shelf, the red on another, the blue on
another… Soon the book stall looked like a
little rainbow! Hello Kitty stood back. That was
MUCH better.

Hello Kitty looked at her watch — it was ten o'clock already! The fair was starting and she still hadn't got back to Dear Daniel, or Tammy, or Fifi! She couldn't leave her stall now with people coming in through the gates. She hoped the others had sorted themselves out!

Her family were coming towards her — there was Mama and Papa, along with Grandma and Grandpa and Mimmy.

Mimmy called out to greet her.

Hello Kitty waved back, and as they came over she noticed Mama was carrying a *perfectly* baked apple pie. Is must be for the competition!

Mama smiled, and told her it was;

what did Hello Kitty think?

Hello Kitty knew **exactly**

what she thought – Mama would

definitely win with that!

Grandma and Grandpa looked around the

stall as they talked. It looked lovely. Grandpa

wanted to be the first person to buy a book,

so he asked where the

books on ships and

battles were.

Ummm…

Hello Kitty had

no idea!

Ooh – and did she have any books on cookery? Grandma wanted to know.

And what about fishing? Papa was looking through all the brightly coloured books for one.

Mimmy wanted an adventure story too!

Hello Kitty felt herself blush, and started to explain. The thing was that the books were organised by colour. So she wasn't sure where the different ones were!

Grandma smiled at her. It was certainly an unusual way to organise a book stall! Hello

Kitty had thought it would look pretty. But maybe it wasn't such a good idea after all.

Grandma gently suggested that it might be easier for people to find the books if they were organised by subject. Maybe they could help her rearrange them? Grandpa nodded — he would help too.

Hello Kitty gasped. That would be

AMAZING! Her friends also needed

some help. Would it please be OK if she left

them there while she went to check if they were

all right, she asked?

Grandpa smiled. That would be absolutely

fine. Mimmy and Mama could serve the

customers, and the rest of

them would help sort

the books. Hello Kitty

smiled and thanked

them all; she was so

lucky to have such a

wonderful family!

She dashed off to see Dear Daniel. His first

customer, a little boy, was looking at himself

in the mirror. He had black stripes all over

his face. His lip was wobbling.

He had wanted to be a

spider – but he looked

more like an alien.

But aliens were super-

cool! Hello Kitty reassured

him quickly, smiling.

The little boy cheered up. He

would be an alien instead! He ran off, making

spaceship noises, and Dear Daniel and Hello

Kitty giggled.

Dear Daniel groaned; face painting was so *hard*. He had been trying to draw a spider and he was good at drawing bugs. What if someone wanted to look like a fairy or a mermaid? They'd probably look like a dragon! Hello Kitty laughed gently. It would be fine; he shouldn't worry, she said.

Dear Daniel looked at her. Please could she do the face painting instead of him, he asked? He could run the book stall for her... *please?*

Before Hello Kitty could reply, Fifi came running over. She and Tammy both needed their help! Tammy with running the castle, and Fifi had loads of people wanting to make models and no model making stuff apart from lots of glue, pipe cleaners and paints. She had *no idea* what people could make with those!

Dear Daniel's eyes lit up. Glue, pipe cleaners and paints? Hmmm. They could get them to...

But just then Miss Davey came hurrying over too, looking

worried. Oh dear; what could have gone wrong now? Miss Davey explained that the balloons that were going to be released hadn't turned up. She didn't know what to do! The day would be spoiled without them.

Fifi gasped.

Oh no!

Dear Daniel gasped too — what a terrible thing to happen.

Miss Davey was disappointed. She had been hoping they'd raise lots of money with them.

Hello Kitty looked at everyone's faces and

took a deep breath. It would be all right; she

was sure they could sort it out. She thought

fast… and suddenly, she had it! There was a

great party shop in town and they delivered

balloons. She had got some when she organised

Mama's birthday party last year. They were

called The Non-Stop Party Shop! They could ring them up, and Hello Kitty was sure they could get there in lots of time for the balloons to be sold and released.

What a great idea! Miss Davey smiled at Hello Kitty. She pulled her phone out; she would call them straightaway.

Hello Kitty turned to the others. Could Dear Daniel take over the model-making stall?

Dear Daniel jumped up. If he could get hold of some paper plates and cups, he could show people how to make model bugs.

Hello Kitty clapped her hands. *Perfect!*

Dear Daniel would get started right away.

He hurried off eagerly.

Fifi would be great at organising the bouncy castle. Hello Kitty suggested she take over from Tammy, and ask her to do the book stall instead. Then Hello Kitty could run the face painting!

Fifi looked delighted.

And now they had balloons! Miss Davey shut her phone. The Non-Stop Party Shop could deliver them within the hour, and it was **all** thanks to Hello Kitty.

Hello Kitty felt a rush of relief. Maybe, just maybe, it was all going to be OK after all!

The Perfect Sleepover

Hello Kitty smiled as she looked across at her

friends that evening. She had thought they'd

all be too tired for a sleepover! Fifi and Dear

Daniel were curled up in their sleeping bags on

her bedroom floor, Tammy was in her bed, and

Hello Kitty had put two armchairs

together to make a place to sleep

herself.

But who could be tired after a day like that!

Everyone agreed that it had been fantastic.

It was true; the fair had been a

great success. The balloons

had arrived and had looked

spectacular when they

were all let go. Hello Kitty had painted faces

all day long, leaving Tammy happily running

the book stall. Fifi had no problem

supervising the bouncy castle

and Dear Daniel had

helped people make model bug after bug. Mama had even won the baking competition for her apple pie! A mountain of money had been raised for the animal rescue centre and Miss Davey had been so pleased with them all that she'd given them specially customised certificates to say thank you.

CERTIFICATE
of
achievement

THIS CERTIFICATE IS
PROUDLY PRESENTED TO

Hello Kitty

for being SUPER-helpful
and saving the day!

It really had been the *perfect* day!

Dear Daniel reached over, and grabbed a list that had fluttered out of Hello Kitty's pocket. What was this, he asked?

Hello Kitty giggled as she tried to grab it back.

Dear Daniel started to read it out to them. It was a sleepover checklist – Hello Kitty was so good at organising things! Hello Kitty blushed

and smiled.

Tammy hugged her. It was great that Hello Kitty was so good at organising things, she said, or they wouldn't

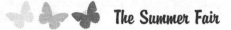
have raised so much money

at the fair!

Fifi was curious;

what was on the list

then? She leaned over

Dear Daniel's shoulder as he read it out.

Dear Daniel started reading again. Bedding,

Movie, Midnight Feast, Breakfast, where

everyone would sleep, the games they would

play… He grinned. Hadn't she forgotten

something?

Hello Kitty couldn't think what it could be!

She leaned over his shoulder and grabbed the

piece of paper.

Fifi knew the answer immediately, and declared it loudly – to invite her friends! That was what was missing. A sleepover wouldn't be a sleepover without friends.

It was true. But Hello Kitty thought they would know that. As she looked around the room at the **happy** faces, she knew there was nowhere else she would rather be.

At that moment, there was a knock at the door and Mimmy came in, carrying a tray of milk and cookies for everyone, with Alice looking in over her shoulder. They were going to be having their own sleepover.

Milk and cookies! Just what they needed.

Hello Kitty thanked her as Mimmy left and
closed the door behind her. The friends all
looked at each other happily. So they had
done it!

Even though Hello Kitty told everyone what

to do,

Tammy was quiet,

Fifi was loud,

And Dear Daniel was sensible!

Hello Kitty smiled. They were all different.

They should have known that and done what

they were good at instead of trying to change

themselves. Things would have been much easier if they'd each done the stalls they liked best from the start! They were so funny.

Fifi had a suggestion. They should agree never to try to change themselves again! In fact, it should be a new **Friendship Club** rule to join the other rules.

What should they write, they all wondered? They thought hard, until Tammy had an idea. What about:

Good friends like you just the way you are!

It was ***perfect!*** Hello Kitty wrote it

down under the other Friendship Club rules.

But there was a whole night ahead of them,

and there was so much to do. What should they

do first? The four friends looked at each other

and grinned. It was time for the sleepover

to begin!

The end

Turn over the page for activities and fun things that you can do with your friends – just like Hello Kitty!

Plan the Perfect Sleepover!

Hello Kitty loves sleepovers, and now you can have one with your own friends – just follow these simple instructions and ideas to make sure you have the best sleepover ever!

Instructions

There are lots of things you need to think about when you're planning a sleepover. Take a look at all these ideas, and follow the checklist on page 104 to make sure you don't forget anything. Always remember to check with Mama and Papa before you invite your friends over to stay!

Who to Invite

Make a list of who you want to invite. Make sure you check with Mama or Papa how many friends can stay before you ask them over!

Where to Sleep

Work out where you will all sleep. Is it in your room, or do you need somewhere bigger, like the living room? Do you have enough beds, or will someone need to sleep on the couch or the floor? Don't forget to tell your friends if they need to bring a sleeping bag!

What to do!

What will you do with your friends when they are over? You can watch a movie, play games, and even have a midnight feast! Make sure you eat an hour or two before you go to sleep though – you don't want to go to bed with a full tummy!

Lights Out

Make sure you keep the noise down when everyone else goes to bed. You don't want to keep the rest of the house awake… even if you can't sleep just yet.

Breakfast

Plan your breakfast menu. Keep it simple if you have lots of friends to feed!

Tidying Up

Once everyone is awake, tidy up everything from the night before, and put away your bedding. If you make sure the room is like it was before the sleepover, you won't have to worry later on.

Morning Madness!

With so many people getting ready you may need to work out a timetable for the morning — especially on a school day. Check the best time to get started and figure out who will go first, so everybody can get ready!

Sleepover checklist

To make things easier, tick off each item
on the sleepover checklist as you do it!

- [ ] 1. Ask permission from Mama or Papa
- [ ] 2. Choose and invite your guests
- [ ] 3. Decide where you'll all sleep
- [ ] 4. Choose your activities for the night – games, movies and feasts!
- [ ] 5. Shhh... Keep the noise down!
- [ ] 6. Plan your breakfast
- [ ] 7. Decide your morning timetable
- [ ] 8. Tidy up!

Hello Kitty and her friends (especially Tammy) love to read! Follow the simple instructions here to make a pretty Hello Kitty bookmark for when you're reading too.

ALWAYS ASK A GROWN-UP FOR HELP BEFORE USING SCISSORS!

You will need:

A piece of thin card (A4 size)

A ruler

Scissors

Coloured pens and pencils

A glue stick

Using your pencil and ruler, cut out a rectangle of card about 6cm wide and 16cm high. Then draw Hello Kitty's head on to the card too, copying the template on page 106, and cut it out!

Draw on Hello Kitty's eyes, nose and bow, and then draw on her whiskers with black pen. Then glue it to the top of your bookmark, and you're ready to decorate! Colour in your bookmark in bright colours – her bow could be red, or any colour you like!

Why not add some glitter and sparkles too? They'll make any story the sparkliest you'll ever read!

Turn the page for a sneak peek at

next adventure...

The Pop Princess

It was Saturday, and Hello Kitty hummed as she
arranged her lip balms in a row and then lined up
her hair bows on her desk. Finally she sorted out her
pens and pencils, putting the pink ones – her favourite
colour – right at the front. There! She sat back. Her
desk looked just right!

She heard the sound of running feet on the landing
and then her bedroom door flew open. Her twin sister
Mimmy burst in, gasping. She looked like she was

about to pop with excitement. What could the good news be?

Mimmy jumped up and down in excitement as she told Hello Kitty that their favourite band in the whole wide world, the Fizzy Pops, were having an open-air concert in the park in two weeks' time and Mama said that they could both go! Hooray!

Hello Kitty grabbed her sister's hands and they spun each other round. The Fizzy Pops were the best pop group ever! This was SUPER news!

Mama had also told Mimmy that they could take a picnic to the concert. She was on the phone right now buying two tickets.

Hello Kitty felt happiness rush through her all the way from her toes to her head. They could make special food and take the big pink and blue picnic rug and dance and sing along with the songs. It would be so much fun! Suddenly she knew what would make it even more fun… what if Fifi, Tammy and Dear Daniel could come too?

Fifi, Tammy and Dear Daniel were her really good friends – such good friends that they had formed a club called The Friendship Club. They had membership cards and a password, and had meetings at each other's houses where they played games and made things. They also thought up rules about friendship. Mimmy didn't join them all the time as she had friends of her own too, but she liked being part of the Friendship Club meetings if she was around.

For the concert it would be the more the merrier,

Mimmy said, smiling – and then her eyes widened.
That had given her a great idea! She told Hello Kitty
about an article she'd read in Pop Girl magazine last
month. It said that sometimes when the Fizzy Pops
performed they chose groups of people from the
audience who were dancing really well to appear on
stage with them...

Find out what happens next in...

Win Hello Kitty Goodies and prizes!

Collect the secret passwords in the first six Hello Kitty and Friends books, and go to **www.harpercollins.co.uk/HelloKittyandFriends** to download your exclusive Hello Kitty activities, games and fun!

Collect all six secret passwords to win super-special goodies!*

Coming soon:

HELLO KITTY STORY
HELLO KITTY
and friends
The Treasure Hunt

A HELLO KITTY STORY
HELLO KITTY
and friends
The Talent Show